The AMAZING ADVENTURES of BATMAN™

THE TERRIBLE TWOS

by **Brandon T. Snider**

illustrated by **Omar Lozano**

Batman created by Bob Kane with Bill Finger

PICTURE WINDOW BOOKS
a capstone imprint

Published by Picture Window Books, an imprint of Capstone.
1710 Roe Crest Drive
North Mankato, Minnesota 56003
www.capstonepub.com

Library of Congress Cataloging-in-Publication Data is available on the
Library of Congress website.
ISBN: 978-1-5158-4823-3 (library binding)
ISBN: 978-1-5158-5882-9 (paperback)
ISBN: 978-1-5158-4828-8 (eBook PDF)

Summary: Batman and his crime-fighting cousin Batwoman are in double
trouble! The super-villain Two-Face is on a crime spree in Gotham City. Who
will win when the super heroes face off against this two-bit crook? Find out
in this action-packed early chapter book for the youngest of readers.

Designer: Kayla Rossow

Printed in the United States of America.
PA100

TABLE OF CONTENTS

Hidden in the shadows,
a hero keeps watch.
He is the Caped Crusader
against crime. He is the
Dark Knight of justice.
These are …

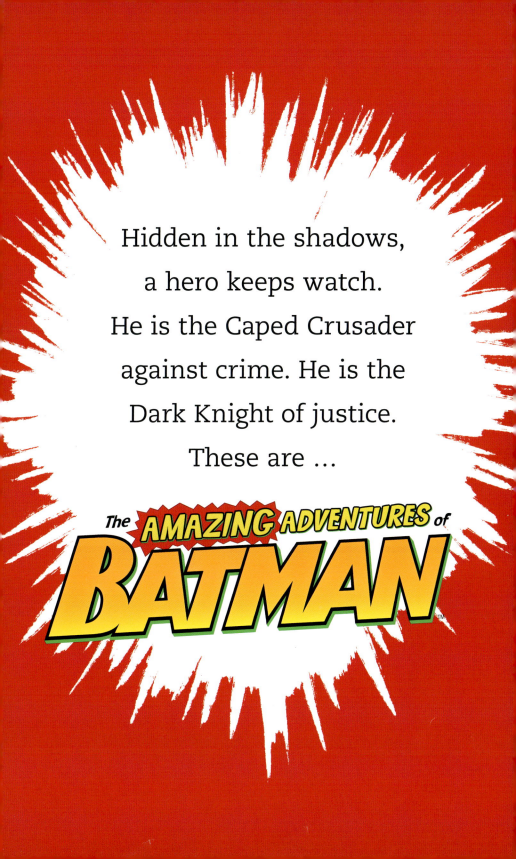

The **AMAZING ADVENTURES** of
BATMAN

CHAPTER 1

BAT-FAMILY

DING DONG!

On the edge of Gotham City, a guest arrives at Wayne Manor. It's Kate Kane, Bruce Wayne's cousin.

The butler opens the door. "Master Wayne is waiting for you," Alfred says. He leads Kate to a nearby elevator.

Kate steps into the elevator. "Luckily, I brought my work clothes," she tells Alfred. Then the metal doors shut.

Inside the elevator, Kate puts on her uniform. She becomes the crime fighter known as Batwoman!

A minute later, the elevator doors open. Batman is waiting for her inside the Batcave.

"We've got trouble," he says.

"I'm here to help," Batwoman replies. "That's what family is for."

The hero leads Batwoman to the Batcomputer. He plays two videos for her.

"In this video, Two-Face is robbing a bank," he explains. "In the other, he's robbing a diamond store . . . at the exact same time."

"How?" Batwoman asks. "He can't be in two places at once!"

Batman points to the video of the bank robbery. "One is the real Two-Face," he says. Then he points to the diamond store video. "The other is a robot."

"Two-Face is daring you to come after him," Batwoman says. "But he won't expect me to show up."

"I'll handle the real Two-Face at the bank," Batman says.

"I'll head to the diamond store to stop the robot," Batwoman adds.

She hops onto the nearby Batcycle. **VROOM! VROOM!**

At the same time, Batman
fires up the Batmobile. "Let's be
careful out there," he says.

Batman steps on the gas and
races away.

ZOOOOM!

Batwoman blasts out of the

Batcave toward the diamond store.

CHAPTER 2

THE CHASE

A short while later, Batwoman arrives at the diamond store.

SMASH! She crashes through the roof! Broken glass flies everywhere.

Two-Face's thugs prepare for a fight.

FWOOSH! Batwoman leaps over the thugs. **BWACK!** She kicks them from behind, knocking the crooks to the ground.

"Stay down," she says. Batwoman spots the Two-Face robot and chases after it.

Batwoman fires a Batrope and swings into the robot's path.

"Not so fast, bolt bag!" she exclaims.

The crook lets out a wicked laugh. Batwoman is shocked. "Surprise!" says the real Two-Face. The villain tricked the heroes by trading places with his robot!

Chapter 3

DOUBLE CROSS

Two-Face holds up a coin

to Batwoman. "Feeling lucky?"

he asks.

The villain flips his coin!

When it lands, Two-Face

quickly shouts, "You lose!"

The villain knocks over a giant cabinet full of diamonds. It topples toward Batwoman.

The hero leaps out of the way just in time. The cabinet crashes to the floor, spilling diamonds across the store.

Two-Face escapes out the back door.

Just then, Batman messages

Batwoman from the Gotham

City Bank. "It looks like Two-Face

tricked us," he says. "I'll be there

soon to help you bring him in."

Meanwhile, Batwoman chases Two-Face into the run-down Gotham City Steelworks. But he's nowhere to be found.

"I know you're in here!" Batwoman shouts.

A creaking sound comes from the rafters above.

 **THOOM!** Two-Face swings a steel

beam in Batwoman's direction.

She hops on top of the beam

and rides it like a surfboard.

FWOOSH!

The beam swings again.

Batwoman leaps onto the

rafters with a thud. Two-Face

can't believe his eyes.

Suddenly, Batwoman

pushes him over the railing.

"Happy landings!" she says.

Two-Face falls into a safety

net! Batman arrived when

Two-Face wasn't looking.

"Surprise!" Batwoman says.

"Feeling *unlucky*, Two-Face?"

"Two-Face didn't plan on two heroes for the price of one," Batman says. "Great teamwork, Batwoman."

"Anytime, Batman," Batwoman replies. "Teamwork is what our amazing adventures are all about."

BATMAN'S
SECRET MESSAGE!

What is Batwoman's full name?

11 1 20 8 5 18 9 14 5
11 1 14 5

Use the code below to solve the
Batcomputer's secret message!

1	2	3	4	5	6	7	8	9	10	11	12	13
A	B	C	D	E	F	G	H	I	J	K	L	M

14	15	16	17	18	19	20	21	22	23	24	25	26
N	O	P	Q	R	S	T	U	V	W	X	Y	Z

butler (BUHT-lur)—a male servant who cares for someone else's house

cabinet (KAB-in-it)—a piece of furniture with shelves and drawers

crook (KRUK)—a criminal

daring (DAIR-ing)—challenging someone to do something

run-down (RUHN-doun)—worn out, or in need of repair

topple (TAHP-uhl)—to fall over

uniform (YOO-nuh-form)—a special set of clothes worn by a particular person or group

villain (VIL-uhn)—a wicked, evil person

wicked (WIK-uhd)—bad or evil

The AMAZING ADVENTURES of

BATMAN ™

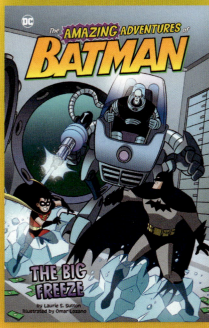

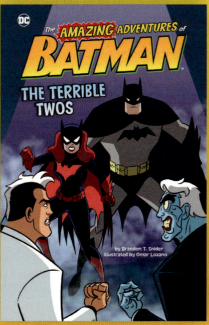

Author

Brandon T. Snider has authored over 50 books featuring pop culture icons such as Captain Kirk, Transformers and the Muppets. Additionally, he's written books for Cartoon Network favorites such as Adventure Time, Regular Show, and Powerpuff Girls. His award-winning *Dark Knight Manual* was mentioned in *Entertainment Weekly*, *Forbes*, and *Wired*. Brandon lives in New York City and is a member of the Writer's Guild of America.

Illustrator

Omar Lozano is an illustrator from Monterrey, Mexico. He has been involved in projects with IDW, Dark Horse, DC and of course Capstone. In his spare time, he likes to watch movies, reading comics and books, play videogames, go out with friends and travel. Can you guess what other hobbies he has? Yeah, to draw and paint.